MW01691499

The Truth I Must Invent

Dear Luz,

Thank you for signing up for the Goodreads giveaway. I hope you enjoy these poems.

All the best,

Francis DiClemente

Francis DiClemente

All Rights Reserved
©2023 Francis DiClemente
Published by Poets Choice & Free Spirit LLC
www.poetschoice.in
First Edition March 2023

Cover Design by Koni Deraz
Cover Photo by Engin Akyurt
Book Design by Adil Ilyas, Pakistan

ISBN: 978-93-95193-73-3
Price: $22.50
BCID: 287-16831497

Acknowledgments

"Cake Mistake" was published in *What We See on Our Journeys: An Anthology of Poetry by Onondaga County Poets* (Willet Press, 2021).

"Looking Through Spindles," "Fingers in Hair," and "Craniopharyngioma (Youthful Diary Entry)" were published in 2021 on the Featured Poets blog, presented by Osamase Ekhator.

"Diagnosis" was published in essay form on the website of The Pituitary Foundation.

"Inner Antipathy" was published on the poetry blog Ephemeral Elegies.

Contents

III.

IV.

V.

VI.

I.

Uncle On Screen

The dead never disappear.
They live on through social media.
My deceased uncle Fiore appears to me
in a surprise party video
posted on Facebook
less than three months before his passing.

He greets his nieces and nephews,
his shrunken figure enveloped in hugs.
At the end of the clip,
at about the eighteen-second mark,
he bobs his head and looks up—
his black eyes penetrating
the glass screen of my computer
and locking on me.

The frozen image is eerie,
but also comforting.
His expression seems to say:
"Hey, I'm still here, even though
I'm on the other side.
Time and space and decomposition
cannot eradicate the bond of love
forged during my lifetime.
I'm still watching you.
And anytime you want to see me,
just log in to FB and hit play."

Bubble in the Bathroom

A soap bubble
rises from
the bathroom sink,
lifts toward
the white ceiling tile,
and then disintegrates,
leaving behind
no liquid residue.

The evaporation is
reminiscent of
the cycle of life—
the bubble
and the body
sharing the physics
of ceasing to be.

Little Spider

All matter clings to life.
Even a tiny brown spider
fights to stay afloat
before it circles the drain.

Halloween Screening

You can't fault
Frankenstein's creature
For what he became.

He never had a choice.
He didn't ask to be born.
He didn't seek existence.

With an abnormal brain
And cobbled parts,
He can't be blamed for
The terror he unleashed.

He was only acting
According to his nature.
The real monster here
Is the man who
Created the creature.

Man Inside *Nighthawks*

I assume I was nothing
before I found myself sitting here,
staring straight ahead.

I can't move my head.
I can't smoke the cigarette
pressed between the fingers
of my right hand or drink the cup
of coffee resting on top of the counter.
I can't touch the woman seated next to me
or talk to the other men in the diner.

This is my life: suspended in warm, yellow light,
trapped in a soundless environment—
no water running, no fan whirring, or grill sizzling.
No sirens or street sounds beyond the glass.

Time drags on with no discernible shift—
no transition to morning.
Here, night never ends.

Yet my mind still works.
In fact, it never stops.
I'm cursed with thoughts that run continuously.

Why am I here?
And where exactly is here?
What purpose do I serve?

Do I have a past? Did I live elsewhere,
before I became frozen in this moment—
captured and imprisoned for eternity?

If only I could talk.
If only I could open my lips and make a sound.
Then I could scream for help.
But who would hear my voice?

If only I could stand up
and walk around,
stretch my legs and
stare outside the window.

But since I can't move,
the composition will remain unaltered,
as I will stay locked in place
inside this painting,
hanging on a gallery wall.

Cake Mistake

Peggy made a huge mistake
when she baked a
grocery store celebration cake.
She put a *D*
where a *T* should be
in the middle of the
word *CONGRATULATIONS.*

The customer was pissed.
But Peggy kept silent
as the irate woman left the store
without paying for her order.

Peggy's manager docked her pay,
and yelled at her for making
such a stupid mistake,
to which Peggy replied:

"Look, I never went to college
and there's no spell-check when baking a cake.
And I'm sorry I screwed up, but I think that *D*
will taste just as sweet as a *T,*
so I'll take that cake home for my kids to eat."

II.

Enchanted Forest

When I was a young boy,
I dreamed of a forest for a backyard.
I wanted to open the sliding glass door
on the bottom floor of our raised ranch home
and step outside, entering a tract of land
with acres and acres of evergreen and deciduous trees.
No neatly trimmed lawn, no tool shed,
no swimming pool, or garden with basil and tomato plants.

I longed for a secret place I could run to and get lost in,
the green canopy shimmering above me
as my feet struck a rocky path
leading deep into the woods.

I created this place in my mind so the cacophony
of screeching woodland birds and hissing insects
would muffle the sound of my parents
screaming on the other side of the drywall.
I made this wish nightly while closing my eyes
and trying not to hear the yelling
coming from the next room.

And when I couldn't fall asleep, I'd pull myself up,
part the navy blue, sailboat-adorned curtains
and look outside my bedroom window—
where, to my dismay, I would see nothing
but a plot of green grass in our backyard.

Looking Through Spindles

I climb out of bed and clutch
the white balusters at the top of the stairs
as harsh words fly behind walls
too thin to hold my parents' rage.

My sister creeps out of her room,
shrugs her shoulders,
and moves toward me in the hallway,
passing the door to the master bedroom.
She sits down next to me
and whispers, "What happened now?"
"I don't know," I say.
And we listen for clues, trying to determine
the cause of the latest fight.

Did Dad come to bed drunk
and make advances on our mother?
Did she recoil or lash out, scratching his eyes?
But we hear no violent action
on the other side of the white door—
only voices laced with acrimony.
And we remain seated on the stairs,
exhausted but unable to fall back asleep.

Zooming out, I see those siblings
in a Polaroid image, sealed under a plastic sheet
in a leather-bound photo album.
And as the adult looking back,
breaking the fourth wall,

I wonder why this memory pricks my brain
when so many others would illuminate my parents'
kindness, decency, and exemplary work ethic.
Why, when I could have chosen from
a myriad of positive scenarios,
does this one seize my attention,
demanding to be chronicled?

My mother and father are both dead
and can't defend their actions.
And I feel riddled with guilt
for tarnishing their memories.
I also understand that the truth
doesn't always tell the full story.
My conscience obligates me to explain that
while Mom and Dad weren't perfect,
they loved us and endured sacrifices
to make our lives a little better.
And while that's a weak way to end a poem,
the wider perspective allows me to
forgive my mother and father for being human—
for being real people and not just my parents.

Aplomb

When I was a kid,
my mother's execution of
the silent treatment
erected a scaffolding of shame.

But her rejection in my youth
produced equanimity in adulthood.

And so I thank her for the mettle
her emotional abuse constructed.

Voiceless

The dead can’t defend themselves
From your incrimination.
They can’t refute what you claim.
And doesn’t your muddled memory
Distort the truth to some degree?

Diagnosis

Dad put the car in park and let it idle,
and as I slid into the passenger seat and adjusted myself,
he leaned over and kissed me on the cheek,
his tan winter coat brushing against the steering wheel.
I felt a trace of his razor stubble against my skin,
and I could smell a faint odor of Aqua Velva or Brut,
combined with cigarette smoke.
The heater hummed, and he lowered the blast of air.
I wondered why we weren't moving yet.
He wasn't crying,
but he appeared on the verge of spilling emotions.

"What's the matter, Dad?" I asked.
"The hospital called your mother today."
He switched on the overhead light,
reached into his jacket pocket,
and pulled out a torn piece of paper.
"Here," he said, handing me the slip of paper,
"This is what they think you have.
I wrote it down, but I don't think I spelled it right."
Scribbled in faint blue ink was a misspelling
of the word "craniopharyngioma."
My father's voice cracked as he said, "It's cranio-phah-reng …
something like that … oh, I don't know,
it's some kind of brain tumor."

I looked at the paper and felt a wave of satisfaction
as my father let out a sigh.
He seemed locked into position in the driver's seat,

unable to shake off the news and go through the motions
of putting the car in gear and driving away.
We clutched hands, and I said, "It's OK, Dad. Don't worry.
But what do we do now? What's next?"
"You have to go back there for more tests," he said.
You may need surgery."
"All right," I said.
He switched off the overhead light,
and we exited the parking lot.
We grew silent inside the car
as we passed the naked trees lining Pine Street
in our city of Rome, New York.

While my father was crestfallen,
I felt elated as I sat in the passenger seat.
The CT scan with contrast had given me a medical diagnosis—
a reason for my growth failure at age fifteen.
It explained why my body had not changed,
why I had not progressed through puberty,
and why I was so different from the other boys my age.
I still considered myself a physical anomaly,
but the tumor proved it wasn't my fault.

That knowledge gave me satisfaction
and a stirring of excitement.
I looked down at the piece of paper again
and studied the word—"craniopharyngioma."
I tried to sound it out in my head while my dad drove on.
I thought the word would roll off my tongue
like poetry if I said it out loud.
Craniopharyngioma. Cranio-Phar-Ryng-Ee-Oh-Mah …
sort of like onomatopoeia.

Craniopharyngioma (Youthful Diary Entry)

Craniopharyngioma gave me
an excuse for being unattractive.
I had a problem inside my head.
It wasn't my fault
I stood four foot eight inches tall
and looked like I was
twelve years old instead of eighteen—
and then nineteen
instead of twenty-four.
I couldn't be blamed for
my sans-testosterone body
straddling the line
between male and female.

The brain tumor
spurred questions
about my appearance,
aroused ridicule,
and provoked sympathy.
I heard voices whispering:
"Guess how old that guy is?"
And, "Is that a dude or a chick?"

And while I waited for my
body to mature, to fall in line,
and to achieve normal progression,
I remember wishing the surgeons
had left the scalpel

inside my skull
before they closed me up,
knitting the stitches
from ear to ear.

I prayed the scalpel
would twist and twirl
while I slept at night—
carving my brain
like a jack-o'-lantern—
splitting the left and right
hemispheres,
and effacing the memory
of my existence.

Syringe Scene

I want to shed adolescence
like a snake sloughs its skin.
But manhood creeps up on me
like osteoporosis or old age.

Masculinity delivered in
1 cc. doses of testosterone
injected into my ass.
Then, like delaying an orgasm,
I hold back.
If I slam the plunger,
the drug won't absorb into the muscle.

I must take my time allowing the
viscous fluid to enter the body—
as the syringe becomes my mate,
in a union between flesh and
the steel tip of the hypodermic needle.

No Change

Late 1980s, Rome, New York—
a boom box blasting
on an outdoor basketball court.

I am reclining on
a red plastic slide,
listening to Michael Hutchence
sing the lyrics to the
INXS song "Don't Change."

I can't resolve my
mixed-up physical state—
a half-boy, half-man
with an amorphous, androgynous body.

There's no resolution
for my situation.
I can't force the
change I need—
to grow, to mature,
to be normal
like everyone else.

A basketball bounces
on the court,
the cassette tape spins,
the next song plays,
and music helps
me to forget

who I am
in this moment—
the person
I haven’t become yet.

Freak Show

Step right up
and see the boy
who never grew up.

Diary Entry: 1994

Dichotomy—
adult and adolescent
at the same time.

The body lies.

Am I a man
if I am
the only one
who knows it?

Retracing the Past

The crinkling of leaves,
And soughing trees,
Frost-caked grass,
And warm breath on glass,
All take me back—
To days elapsed,
To a time that tested
The courage of a soul
Still being formed.

The tumor thwarting growth,
The *boy* tightening his hold,
The *man* kept incognito,
Shrouded in diffidence,
Abandoning his insurrection,
Striving for acceptance,
And yearning for a love
That would never come.

Freeing the Prisoner

I feel like a foreigner in my body,
a prisoner of my skin—
the man within held hostage
by the outer shell of a boy.

I want to murder myself—
kill the odd, ugly figure
dressed in boy's clothes,
and release the man inside
so he can live free
somewhere else.

Fission

The exterior boy was unwilling
to let the man inside come out.
Only one face and body
could be shown to the world,
and the boy retained control.

Time and pharmaceuticals
ended this conflict,
the man emerging—
breaking through the shell
and scattering the fragments
of the boy on the sidewalk.

With the twin beings cleaved,
only one figure remained—
the man I became.

III.

Friction

A reckoning with reality—
succumbing to the
necessity of survival
in a day-to-day grind
that abrades the soul
and disperses the flecks.

Fertile Ground

A malignant root
bears a bitter fruit,
and loneliness derides
like cancer thrives.

Inertia

Words unspoken and stakes not wagered—
nailed-down desires scar over with time,
when puppy love is collared by silence,
or prom night is spent sitting at home—
replaying missed opportunities in comforting quiet.

Wrong Number

My only human contact today
comes by mistake—
when a woman calls me
looking for someone else.

Ending All Attempts

I have stopped
bemoaning the memory
of unreciprocated affection.

The Cave

I claw
at the walls
of the cave
I call home.

Tentacles

I must free myself
from myself—
remove the fingers
from around my throat.

Inner Antipathy

I want to be
someone other
than me.

I look
in the mirror,
and my face
incites enmity.

Echo Inside

What must I do
to overcome myself?
To finally evolve
into someone else?

The Story of a Face

Why torment myself
about physical features
I can't control or alter?

I didn't construct
this face.
I didn't fuck up
the blueprints.
That design flaw
rests with God.

But I must never forget—
my eyes, nostrils,
and mouth are
in the right place—
and I can see,
smell, breathe, and speak.

My ugliness
does not interfere
with the functions
of my face.

The Gulf

The chasm of despair lies open—
the gulf between myself and other people exposed.
In this cavern, I search for a glimmer of hope,
a solitary beam of light
to penetrate the blackened hole.

Outsider

I am marooned on a tropical island,
making sandcastles to pass the time.
I am adrift on the ocean,
floating on the blue waves,
untrammeled by marine life.

I am a man apart from others,
one who remains habitually estranged,
residing on the surface,
never burrowing deeper,
the fine root exposed to the elements.

Mattress Moment

You don't get to cry
"No Fair"
Mr. Hyman Roth.

This is the life
you have chosen.

You don't get to pine
for your salad days,
whatever the fuck that means.

You don't get to
flip over the mattress
on the bed you've made.

The Wanting is the Hardest Part

Tom Petty was wrong.
The waiting isn't the hardest part.
The wanting is the hardest part.

Wanting fucks everything up—
wanting a better job, a better marriage,
a better house, a better life.
That seed of desire fucks with your head,
makes you think you can be something you're not.

What if I discarded desire? What if stopped wanting?
What if I no longer sought a better life?
Can I let go of that fantasy
and accept who I am right now,
without seeking a better version of myself—
the idealized me I hold inside my head?

Camera Angle

What would I choose
if I were given a chance
to lead a different life?

What mistakes
would I correct?
What new road
would I take?

But you can't splice
the scenes of your life
to edit the past.
You can only point
the camera forward
and zoom into the future.

No Substitute

I must contend
with the discontent
I wrestle with
in a life I despise
but cannot supplant.

Acceptance of Dissatisfaction

Did I curse myself with my aspirations?
Did I imprison myself by seeking
the life I desired—only to realize
it wasn't what I wanted?

And now it's too late.
Now I can't go back,
can't return to the place
before my mistakes
led me to where I'm at.

So now I'm stuck with myself,
molded by my failed decisions—
boxed in and destined to live
with my dissatisfaction.

Resolution

You must
Live the life
You have

And not
The one
You want.

IV.

Verbal Parenthood

I gather my children—
words and verses—
put them in a box
we call a poem,
and hope they
will flourish.

Inspired by Beckett

If you are a writer,
And your writing sucks,
Write some more until
Your writing sucks less.

Cursor Flashing

Who wants my words?
Who cares what I write?

Am I deluding myself
by sitting at this computer
every morning and typing
sentences that get saved
and then ignored?

Yet here I am again—
still banging on the keyboard,
still trying to fill the
white space on the screen.

For now, the cursor blinks,
and I'll let that be
the ending of this poem.

Formula for Poetry

Lines on a page
adding up to nothing.

And we call it poetry,
because that nothing

is still something
that did not exist before.

Words Captured

A sentence came to me
in the middle of the night.
I chased down the words
before they slipped
from my brain.

Once captured,
they obeyed my command,
giving up their will to
form the lines of this poem.

But now on the page,
the words look and sound forced.
So I will break them apart—
setting them free
by hitting the *delete* key.

And maybe they can
find a new home
inside another poem.

Poetry Involuntary

In my case,
poetry is involuntary.
I don't write poetry.
Poetry writes itself for me.

A Poet’s Work

The challenge
of placing one word
in front of another—
forming lines of verse
expressing lucidity.

To Edit or Not

Poetry demands precision.
It requires you to nitpick—
to identify and fix
the flaws in your copy,
or else abandon revision
and celebrate the inconsequence
of your mistakes—
since no one's reading
this shit anyway.

V.

Somebody

Every person is worthy of love.
When you look up
and see somebody on the street,
just think—
someone out there
cares if that somebody
comes home tonight.

Fat Man Walking

God loves the obese man
walking on the street.
He doesn't penalize
the man for his girth.
That's because size
is insignificant
to the creator
of the universe.

Body fat and
waist circumference
hold little value
when the gaze
is directed inward—
where it belongs,
beyond the flesh,
to the place where
the soul lives.

Woman Walking

The breasts have a heart
and the buttocks a brain.

I must train my eyes
to look at the whole woman
and not just the parts—

to respect the person
who dwells inside the frame.

Empathy Required

Who knows another person's story?
Who knows the sorrow they endure?
What measure of empathy
can we call forth within ourselves
to see other people
as more than objects to ignore?

Map of Life

I'm living in reverse,
with counterclockwise
timelines circling
inside my brain.

Memories like
pinpricks of light
dotting a map,
diagraming my journey,

showing the points
where my
course diverged,
and I left alternate
lives behind
in the dust.

Looking at
the map
from above,
I see what
I sought
and what
I reaped,
and where
I ended up,

questioning
if this was

the right life—
asking myself
if I followed
the correct path.

Destination

I am here—
planted
in this place.

So I'll make
the best of it.
I'll drive a stake
in the ground
and put up a
big *Welcome* sign,

convincing myself
that this was the journey,
and the destination
I had planned all along.

Yeah, right.
These are the lies I
need to believe,
and the truth I must invent.

A Sky Free of Cloud Congestion

Three o'clock in the morning—
a man standing in a parking lot,
looking up at a sky free of cloud congestion,

contemplating his lack of purpose
in a life he can neither
sever nor alter for better.

So he's stuck in between
the here and the hereafter.
And do you know what that's called?
That's called living like the rest of us.

So he resolves to stop looking up
at the sky for answers,
to stop seeking something
better than what he possesses right now,
in this moment of recognition.

He decides he will start living
unburdened by the weight
of his hopes, wishes, and ambitions.

Hit By Bus

Maybe getting hit by a bus
Wouldn't be such a bad thing.
Over in an instant.
All worries erased.

No time to think—
No time to count
The regrets, the failures,
And the risks you never took.

Reality

After you die,
life goes on
uninterrupted—
because it must.

And with each
passing day,
the memory
of your presence
becomes fainter,

until you
are forgotten,
and the absence of
your existence ignored.

Bird Observation

A seagull fluttering
In the wind,
Intent on adhering
To some preordained
Flight pattern.

Wings outstretched
Above a traffic light—
How pretty the bird looks
Center framed in my windshield.

Witness

I look up as a group of birds
circles buildings in downtown Syracuse.
I resist the urge to pull out my cellphone
and snap a picture for Instagram.

Instead, I hold my gaze skyward,
letting the wind swirl around my face
and the rain patter my forehead,
as the birds duck in unison
behind a limestone structure—
the moment preserved nowhere except in my mind.

No pictures retained or sound recorded.
No trace of the birds in digital form.
And I think that's the point, that's life—
a collection of these impromptu glimpses of existence,
built into a collage, a kaleidoscope of images
demanding attention when presented.

VI.

Paternity

It's a strange coincidence
that my son looks a little like me—
same brown hair,
same brown eyes,
similar face,
and comparable ears
jutting out to the side.

At first glance
you might think
we're related.
But we share no blood,
since I am not his biological father.
The daddy credit belongs
to the man who
donated his sperm
at the fertility clinic.

But lack of
physical connection
does not strip away
my parenthood.
The bond of love
between boy and man
certifies my fatherhood.

Being a Dad

Being a dad
means improvisation.
It means peeing in the sink
when your wife and son
monopolize the only bathroom
in the apartment.

Being a dad
means admitting
you don't
know the answers,
can't figure out the solutions,
don't have a fucking clue
how to stop that kid from crying.

Being a dad
means living with less—
less money, less time,
less sleep, less sex.

Being a dad
means loving
your child
even when you feel
exhausted and aggravated.

Being a dad
means doing
your best every day,

but accepting the failure
built into the equation
of marriage and parenthood.

Being a dad
means being grateful
for the gift
of being a dad.

Straw Surgery

"You did it,
now live with it."
That's the statement
I shout to my
three-year-old autistic son
when he can't
retrieve the
straws he jammed
inside the frame
of a box fan.

But his mom
has a more
generous spirit.
She grabs
kitchen tongs
and performs
"emergency surgery,"
retrieving the straws
while stating the obvious—
which I tend to forget:
"Hey, listen,
he's just a kid."

Bedtime

Eventually, I'll fall asleep,
but until then my kid
keeps annoying me,

flicking on the bedroom light
and screaming incoherent phrases—
bits of songs that make
some sense inside his mind.

Telling him "shh" does no good,
and I can't decipher the words he speaks,
but I do enjoy hearing the sounds they make
when they escape his mouth,
as I close my eyes and try to get some sleep.

Sleepy Time

In bed at night,
curtains fluttering
in front of the
opened window,
and box fan whirring,
creating white noise.

My son recites the alphabet,
screeches a few meows,
and curls up against
my shoulder blades.

But he's not
ready to sleep yet.
Sandwiched between
his parents,
he wriggles,
then moves from a
seated positioned,
to jumping up and down,
to stretching across
our bodies.

The digital alarm clock
shows 12:04—
past midnight,
a new day
ushered in.
Even with

sleep deprivation,
I'm thankful
for being
granted another
twenty-four hours to spend
with my kid.

And I say to him,
"Now that's enough.
Lay down.
It's time to go to sleep."
But my words are futile.

Laughter and Life

The sound of my
autistic son giggling—
his shrills piercing the air.

I laugh along with him,
joining in the mirth,
even if I don't know
what he finds so funny.

Crying at Bedtime

Nothing prepares a parent
for the tantrums of an autistic child.
There's no well of patience to draw from.
You adapt. You divert. You distract.
You do whatever it takes to calm the child down—
until you earn that blessed moment of peace,
when his eyelids drop and he drifts off to sleep,
his small body folded in the cradle of your arms.

Fingers in Hair

I run my fingers through
my son's tangled mop of brown hair
as he lies next to me in bed.
It's 4:30 a.m. and we can't fall asleep.

He waves his hands in front of his eyes,
making stimming motions,
and I imagine his head slamming
against the windshield,
a spiderweb crack forming
in the sheet of glass and
blood pouring from
an opening in his skull.

I press my hand to his head
to try to stop the bleeding,
but the crimson liquid
slips through my fingers
and stains the carpet
and fabric seat covers.

I am reminded of a
Gospel passage (Luke 12:7 NIV):
"Indeed, the very hairs
of your head are all numbered."

I hold some of my son's hairs
in my hand and realize
I cannot prevent a

car accident, fall, gunshot wound,
or disease from killing my son.
I can't prolong or preserve his life.
I can only love him while he still lives.

His hands whip in front of his face,
and he prattles phrases
only he understands.
I bury my fingers deeper
into the mound of his hair and whisper,
"Come on now, sleepy time, Colin."

Autism Sleeps

My son sleeps,
curled under a blanket
on the couch.

His outbursts have ceased.
His cries and screams quieted.
His stimming stopped.

It's like his autism
is in remission.
In sleep, he becomes
like any other child.

Observation After Eating Out

Pity for my son swells.
Yet I feel helpless,
Unable to intervene
To make his autism
Go away.

Our patience dwindles
As his outbursts intensify.
But love does not wane.
Instead, it grows stronger.

I have only one son.
Yes, he is different.
He is noisy and
Requires constant attention.
But I am thankful for
His presence in my life.
And who needs the quiet anyway?

Autism Acceptance

You can't wish away autism.
You can't expect normalcy.
You must accept the boy as he is—
Knowing he may never change.
And that's OK.
Because the child you have
Is a blessing bestowed.

About The Author

Francis DiClemente is an Emmy Award-winning filmmaker who lives in Syracuse, New York. He is the author of multiple poetry collections, most recently *Outward Arrangements: Poems* (independently published, 2021) and *Dreaming of Lemon Trees: Selected Poems* (Finishing Line Press, 2019). His blog can be found at francisdiclemente.com.

Other Poets' Choice Authors

Mr Daydream by Diana Willand
Funnel To Freedoms Ring By Andre Brewer
Its Not About You by Jeremiah Valentine
Soft Reflection by Jamie Lim
Where Have All The Bluejays Gone by Jennifer Ayala
Sunlight Reflector by Sarah Cross
Whispers In The Wind by Echo Quinn
Questions We Didn't Ask Out Loud by Mars Hetherson
Walking Through The Four Seasons by Eugene Stelzig
Serving Sweet Tea by Lisa Kendrick
Dispelling The Clouds by Rivka Conway
Summers In Laurel Canyon by Spencer J. Vigil
Burnout by Jeff Kimball
Whispers of Daydreams by April Federico
Unheard Whispers by Dianne C. Braley
The After by Terry Dawson
Joys Of Seasons By Paula M. Rodriguez
Free Air Berlin by Richard Eric Johnson
Homelessness by Crystal Barker
Seasoned Women by Cathy Hollister
Blunder Down Under By Christopher Mardiroussian

Dear Reader,

We are ecstatic to note that you chose to read one of our publications. The time you invested in reading this book is much appreciated. We value your allegiance. As a give-back present, we will be happy to share 'YOUR PICTURE HOLDING THIS BOOK' on our Official Social Media Handles such as Facebook, Instagram, and Twitter. (add comma after Instagram) All you have to do is – send it to us.

1. Write Your Name
2. Review, if any
3. Subject Line of Email – Pic Holding Book (Book Name)
4. Image Attached – jpeg / gif/ png file.

Email it to – poetschoice@hotmail.com